MR. GREEDY

by Roger Hargreaves

WORLD INTERNATIONAL

Mr Greedy liked to eat!

In fact Mr Greedy loved to eat, and the more he ate the fatter he became.

And the trouble was, the fatter he became the more hungry he became.

And the more hungry he became the more he ate.

And the more he ate the fatter he became.

And so it went on.

Mr Greedy lived in a house that looked rather like himself.

It was a roly-poly sort of a house.

One morning Mr Greedy awoke rather earlier than usual.

He'd been dreaming about food, as usual, and that had made him wake up feeling hungry, as usual.

So Mr Greedy got up, went downstairs and ate the most enormous breakfast.

This is what Mr Greedy had for his breakfast.

TOAST – 2 slices

CORNFLAKES – 1 packet

MILK – 1 bottle

SUGAR – 1 bowlful

TOAST – 3 slices

EGGS – 3 boiled

TOAST – 4 slices

BUTTER – 1 dish

MARMALADE – 1 pot

When he had finished his enormous breakfast, Mr Greedy sat back in his chair, smiled a very satisfied smile, and thought.

"That was a delicious breakfast," he thought to himself. "Now I wonder what would be nice to have for lunch?"

He decided in order to work up an appetite for lunch he would go for a long walk.

That morning Mr Greedy walked and walked and walked.

Then he discovered a cave.

"That's funny," he thought, "I don't remember seeing that there before."

Mr Greedy, being a curious sort of a fellow, decided to explore.

He entered the dark cave.

Inside he discovered some giant steps leading upwards.

Mr Greedy, being a curious sort of a fellow, decided to climb them.

They were very steep and very difficult to climb, but with much huffing and puffing Mr Greedy climbed up and up.

At the top of the steps Mr Greedy came to a door.

It was, without doubt, the biggest door that Mr Greedy had ever seen. And it wasn't quite shut.

Mr Greedy, being a curious sort of a fellow, decided to see what was on the other side of that door.

So Mr Greedy squeezed himself through the crack in the door, and there before him was an amazing sight.

The biggest room in the world!

The floor was as big as a field.

The table in the middle of the floor was as big as a house, and the chairs around it were as high as trees.

Mr Greedy felt very small.

Then he sniffed.

Coming from somewhere up on top of that gigantic table was the most delicious foody smell that Mr Greedy had ever smelled.

Mr Greedy sniffed again, and then decided that he must get up on to that table, so he began to climb up the leg of the enormous chair.

It was very difficult and it took him a long time, but eventually Mr Greedy stood on the table.

Everything was larger than life.

The salt and pepper pots were both as big as pillar boxes.

There was a bowl of fruit on the table, and Mr Greedy tried to lift one of the oranges.

And Mr Greedy, being Mr Greedy, took a bite out of one of the apples there.

Then he looked around.

Over on the other side of the table stood the source of that delicious smell.

A huge enormous gigantic colossal plate, and on the plate huge enormous gigantic colossal sausages the size of pillows, and huge enormous gigantic colossal potatoes the size of beachballs, and huge enormous gigantic colossal peas the size of cabbages.

Mr Greedy hurried across the table towards the plate, and, being Mr Greedy, began to eat.

Suddenly a shadow fell across the plate, and Mr Greedy found himself being picked up by a giant hand and looking into the eyes of a real live giant.

"AND WHO," thundered the giant, "ARE YOU?"

Mr Greedy was so frightened that he could only just manage to squeak his name. "Mr Greedy," he squeaked.

The giant laughed a laugh as loud as thunder. "GREEDY BY NAME AND GREEDY BY NATURE," he bellowed. "WELL I THINK MR GREEDY THAT YOU NEED TO BE TAUGHT A LESSON!"

And what a lesson it was.

The giant made Mr Greedy eat up everything on that huge enormous gigantic colossal plate.

When he had finished Mr Greedy felt very ill indeed, as if he would burst at any minute.

"Now," said the giant in a much quieter voice, "do you promise never to be greedy again?"

"Oh yes," moaned Mr Greedy, "I promise!"

"Very well," said the giant, "then I'll let you go."

Mr Greedy climbed down from the table and went out through the door feeling very fat and extremely miserable.

And do you know, from that day to this, Mr Greedy has kept his promise.

And do you know something else as well?

Mr Greedy doesn't look like he used to look any more.

He now looks like this, which I think suits him a lot better, don't you?

So if you know anybody who's as greedy as Mr Greedy used to be you know what to tell them, don't you?

Beware of giants!

MORE SPECIAL OFFERS
FOR MR MEN AND LITTLE MISS READERS

In every Mr Men and Little Miss book like this one, and now in the Mr Men
sticker and activity books, you will find a special token. Collect six tokens and we
will send you a gift of your choice
Choose either a Mr Men or Little Miss poster, **or** a Mr Men or Little Miss
double sided full colour bedroom door hanger.

turn this page **with six tokens per gift required** to:
Marketing Dept., MM / LM, World International Ltd.,
PO Box 7, Manchester, M19 2HD

|— 100 mm —|

our name:_____ Age: _____

ddress: _____

_____

_____Postcode: _____

arent / Guardian Name (Please Print)_____

250 mm

ENTRANCE FEE
3 SAUSAGES

MR. GREEDY

ease tape a 20p coin to your request to cover part post and package cost

enclose six tokens per gift, and 20p please send me:-

Collect six of these tokens
You will find one inside every
Mr Men and Little Miss book
which has this special offer.

osters:-   Mr Men Poster   ☐ Little Miss Poster ☐

oor Hangers - Mr Nosey / Muddle ☐ Mr Greedy / Lazy ☐

Mr Tickle / Grumpy ☐ Mr Slow / Busy ☐

20p   Mr Messy / Quiet ☐ Mr Perfect / Forgetful ☐

L Miss Fun / Late ☐ L Miss Helpful / Tidy ☐

L Miss Busy / Brainy ☐ L Miss Star / Fun ☐

Please Tick Appropriate Box

1
TOKEN

tick 20p here please

e may occasionally wish to advise you of other Mr Men gifts.
ou would rather we didn't please tick this box ☐

Offer open to residents of UK, Channel Isles and Ireland only

Full colour Mr Men and Little Miss Library Presentation Cases in durable, wipe clean plastic.

NEW

In response to the many thousands of requests for the above, we are delighted to advise that these are now available direct from ourselves, for only **£4.99** (inc VAT) plus 50p p&p.

The full colour boxes accommodate each complete library. They have an integral carrying handle as well as a neat stay closed fastener.

Please do not send cash in the post. Cheques should be made payable to **World International Ltd. for the sum of £5.49** (inc p&p) per box.

Please note books are not included.

Please return this page with your cheque, stating below which presentation box you would like,

Mr Men Office, World International
PO Box 7, Manchester, M19 2HD

Your name:_____

Address: _____

_____

_____Postcode: _____

Name of Parent/Guardian (please print):_____

Signature:_____

I enclose a cheque for £_____ made payable to World International Ltd.,

Please send me a Mr Men Presentation Box ☐

Little Miss Presentation Box ☐

(please tick or write in quantity)
and allow 28 days for delivery

Thank you

Offer applies to UK, Eire & Channel Isles only